MINORITY
SCHIZOPHRENIC

This is the first book by Michael Avery.

Michael Avery

MINORITY SCHIZOPHRENIC

Minority Left   *New York*

Published by Michael Avery and Minority Left

Cover design by J.D. Malbon

ISBN#: 978-0-578-06794-0

Manufactured in the United States of America

First edition

This novella is a work of fiction.

CONTENTS

ACKNOWLEDGMENTS   XIII

PUBLISHED 2007 INTRODUCTION   XV

1ST UNPUBLISHED 2007 INTRODUCTION   XVII

2ND UNPUBLISHED 2007 INTRODUCTION   XXV

OVERTURE   3

ADRIANA   3

12 DECEMBER 2006   5

TORTURE – PRISON   6

INSCRUTABLE PETE   11

WHO YOU WAITING FOR?   14

YOU SHOULDN'T BE HERE   16

O MAMA, WHERE ART THOU?   17

I, TIRESIAS   17

WOMAN   18

THEY ARE COMING   19

"HOW DID YOU GET HERE?" – A DREAM   20

WHO WAS I TALKING TO?   22

"YOU SHOULDN'T KNOW THAT"   24

SCHIZOMANIA   25

TECHNIQUE   26

YOU ARE OBJECTIFIABLE   27

DOCUMENTATION FOR WRITING STYLE   28

JIMI HENDRIX   29

TEMPLE OF ROBIN HOOD   32

PROPOSE SPACE TRAVEL   33

MARIA   36

JACK   41

FATHERS AND SONS   43

MINORITY SCHIZOPHRENIC   45

MINORITY RISING   49

NARCESSUS   52

COLOR BLIND   52

THE STRUGGLE FOR...HAPPINESS?   54

ASTRO BOY   56

MRS   59

O & E   61

RECKONING DAY   63

HELLO MAMA   65

LET GO MY EGO   67

LAST WORDS OF ADRIAN FRANCIS FARMER 67

EPILOGUE, EPILOGUE   68

Acknowledgments

First, I would like to thank my family, friends, teachers, and colleagues, both past and present, who have helped me arrive at where I am today. Second, I would like to thank Sara McAulay, creative writing instructor, who helped me see more clearly as a writer. And third, thanks to Steve Gutierrez, thesis advisor, who allowed this project to happen, and who above all, encouraged me to Write.

Last but not least, thanks to J.D. Malbon, old friend, for cover design and artwork.

Published 2007 Introduction

This is the story of Adrian Francis Farmer. His story might well be titled, "The Short Unhappy Life of Adrian Francis Farmer," but I settled on *MINORITY SCHIZOPHRENIC* because he is schizophrenic and, therefore, a member of a minority population. Schizophrenics are said to comprise less than 1% of the total population of Earth.

The story takes place roughly between early December 2006 and early spring 2007. When I say takes place, I mean that the story was revealed to me during this period. The actual "story" encompasses Adrian's entire life, but his existence was only made clear to me during the above mentioned dates.

I have tried to keep the story true to Adrian and the way he wanted to be remembered.

Michael Avery
Oakland, CA
May 2007

1st Unpublished 2007 Introduction

This piece, *Minority Schizophrenic*, has undergone many working titles: *Title This Whatever You Like, Dig, Minority Rising, The Daily News*. I changed my mind frequently and never was sure what was right. I settled on *Minority Schizophrenic* because that is the title I dreamt up that most describes the character about which this story is written. He is a minority schizophrenic.

Gentle Reader, there is no time. No time. Time running down. Time running out. Can't slow down.

Gentle Reader, there are only minutes left to go, and I am charged with making my story make sense to you.

I want to. I alternate between violent anger and unbridled compassion.

This story is the culmination of _____.

There are only minutes left to go. I will attempt.

Here's how it started.

Schizophrenia affects less than 1% of people of Earth today. So what? That means that less than 1% of the people, and that's a significant number, suffer the symptoms of schizophrenia which can include hallucinations and paranoia.

How does that relate to me and the story I am about to present to you?

This story is about a young man who is schizophrenic and subject to auditory hallucinations. You will witness some of the things he goes through as a consequence of his condition. He will see his progress through various phases of feelings. You will observe his ultimate decision of what to do with himself because of his condition.

I don't have time to show you what you may want to see. I have spent my entire life in desperate research. I have but only a few minutes to present my findings to you. I realize that many in my audience may not be pleased by my subsequent actions and I find it regrettable that I cannot please everyone.

Gentle Reader, please do not ask me to show-don't-tell you my story. No, while it is possible to describe his life and adventures in full color palette, it is much easier 21 March 2007 to scoot on down to a local cinema and see it for real on screens 30 feet tall. Everything you possibly can imagine. It might as well be real. Matinees cheaper!

What do I want to share with you about me, the author, and what do you want to know about me? The answer to the first is nothing, and the answer to the second is I don't know. I assume if you are reading this it is because you are friend in which case you probably know more about me than I assume. I can't imagine why anyone else would read this, but if he or she discovers this and reads, then he or she may want to know something or everything about me.

The latter is, of course, impossible.

So I will negotiate with you and say something.

Although I am not schizophrenic, I am definitely an auditory person. I live and learn by listening. I cannot prove this other than to say I often remember things that I hear and I really never cared much for visuals.

It does not matter to me much to show anything. I only want to tell my story. I am stubborn. I am sometimes angry. I want to do things my way.

One of the working titles of this piece was *Dig*. Dig is what the old cats used to say to each other when they wanted recognition that their message was heard. That is, "You dig what I'm saying?" My entire purpose in this piece is simply to communicate the state of being of my protagonist. Dig?

I am not concerned with conforming to any pre-established standards of right and wrong based on popular consensus. Dig?

Someone once said that Hemingway's talent was not for metaphor; hence, she did not go to Hemingway for beauty in metaphors. Dig?

Please bear in mind that I hear things. I am more musical than visual or athletic.

Someone once said that an author ought not to be judged for purposes he never intended. Dig?

I could outline the story for you in detail, but it would be tedious and is really not necessary. The entire form of this novella derives from *Naked Lunch*, and anyone with an understanding of how that book works ought to see a comparable form here. Obviously, it is not linear as are traditional narratives.

William S. Burroughs created *Naked Lunch* over the course of several years, mostly while he lived in Tangiers. He was often drug addicted at that time, although I have never really found out if he was intoxicated while he wrote. I have read him say that writing while high is very difficult and not very often fruitful. This makes sense to me, and regardless of whether or not *Naked Lunch* was written while high, Allen Ginsburg and Jack Kerouac definitely helped him assemble the various pieces of the book and put it in coherent order. Ginsburg eventually helped him publish the book and was the main proponent of its defense in the United States book banning trial.

I wrote and have assembled *Minority Schizophrenic* myself under mostly favorable conditions, although I cannot account for why this was the case.

There are many themes in *Minority Schizophrenic*. I cannot postulate a "Trigonometry of Need" or "Calculus of Reality" to quantify my theories. Under these time constraints, hopefully the work speaks for itself.

The story ends with the schizophrenic young man making a permanent life-altering decision. Decisions of these types are final, and they change a person forever.

If I could, I would make you see what I see and understand what I understand, and I can already hear your voice saying, "Yes, Mr. Avery, make me understand." I understand this. It is the writer's job.

But there simply isn't enough time. My hero has already made his life altering decision, and as the Eagles sing, "I'm already gone." I could spend my life trying to make you see what I see and understand what I understand and it may or may not be good enough. I have already spent a lot of my life trying to please other people.

This is the best that I can do.

I started this story in December of 2006. But of course the history is much more complicated than that. I began keeping a journal in my 16th year upon the advice of a counselor whom I was visiting at the time. He suggested I write down my thoughts and feelings as a way to release my tensions. I can remember the night I started – I lay on the floor of my bedroom – I think I was sleeping on the floor for some reason at that time – and I turned on a small desk lamp and began writing in my journal. I did not know what writing was at the time. I hated writing in school and I did not understand anything about it. But as I wrote how I felt, I felt better. It did provide a visceral release.

I became addicted and wrote off and on until the present time whereupon I am still addicted. Writing a journal for me is a visceral experience. I do not do it as an exercise or for a purpose at all. I literally feel a tension

inside my body and writing provides a release the way that
unknotting a hose allows the water to flow. I repeat the
activity much the way a drug user repeats his drug use. I
do it for kicks.

I once asked a friend of mine who is a musician if
he would continue to write songs without an audience. I
believe he said no. Would I write in a journal if at the end
of my life there were to be burned and never viewed by
another soul? Of course. It is a selfish activity and I do it
for me. The reward is doing it just like the addict knows
that the reward of doing drugs is the high of the drug. The
junky does not do drugs for any other purpose. He likes the
high.

My deal was that I never looked at what I wrote. I
wrote and wrote, but I didn't read it. So the piles grew
higher.

And then writing to myself wasn't enough anymore.
I wanted to make something of myself. When I finally
decided to write for an audience, I did not fully understand.
I did not know how to do it. I basically wrote the same
way I always did, but instead showed it to other people.

So, I took workshops and joined writing groups.

But it was in Professor McAulay's class that a
breakthrough finally came. I had written and shared a story
that I felt pretty good about. Its strongest point in my
opinion was the dialogue that I posed between a boyfriend
and a girlfriend. Dialogues, I felt, were my strongest suit
because I can hear them in my head.

The entire point of the story was to communicate
the experience of being locked in a jail of sorts. The hinge
of the story was the "click" of the door that the protagonist
heard behind him when he walked through. He knew
without seeing it or even being told that he was locked, he
was fucked, and there was nothing he could do about it. It
was important to me as an author, and I believe that anyone

who has ever been locked up against their will would identify with an experience like that. I don't know if I can properly explain in words the feeling of not being able to leave a building under any circumstances. Hundreds of thousands of inmates who have come before and will come after me could describe the feeling better.

After the story met with mediocre at best reception from the class and Professor McAuley, she said, "It's OK. There are some strengths here. But it falls short. I don't really know what I'm supposed to take away from this story."

Have you ever tried for something really hard, I mean put your heart into it, and had someone tell you, I'm not getting it? She continued by asking, "So tell me Mike, what were you trying to do here?" I considered the question and then answered in a direct way. I said something like, "The story is about a guy going through a breakdown with his girlfriend who then ends up in a jail against his will until he walks through a door, hears the click, and suddenly realizes that his world has changed forever. Everything depends on the click," I said.

Professor McAulay looked at my story and then looked at me and said, "It didn't work," with finality. I think she carried on with some kind words about "try again and maybe put this part in the front and take this part out" etc., but I was gone already. It took me a few days to realize, but it sunk in that what I was endeavoring to do was not working. I was giving the gold in my heart away in my sincerest possible way, on the sterling silver platter of my experience, with red roses and baby's breath and my beating heart besides, and my audience was telling me, "It doesn't work."

Lucky for me I had already received enough rejection in my life in other ways to be able to recover. I decided at that point to go another way.

I purposely lost my way and unconsciously began *Minority Schizophrenic* which feels like the first work I have ever really written.

My favorite singer says, "You've got to lose your way to find it."

I am not bitter.

I am happy.

Michael Avery
Oakland, CA
May 2007

2nd Unpublished 2007 Introduction

After reading this story, one might make the connection that the author has suffered from influence from the late William S. Burroughs. That would be a correct supposition, and I would agree to plead guilty.

Although it has been said that imitation is the sincerest form of flattery, this is no imitation. I have genuinely been infected with the Burroughsian style, and the reason is simple: His work spoke to me.

I read my first serious set of books when I around 10 or 11, and it was at that time that I learned of the power of literature. What excited me most about the written word was its ability to express beautiful, adventurous, or exciting thoughts and ideas to a reader. I marveled that such a thing could be accomplished.

I read off and on and eventually majored in English in college, but it was the work of Burroughs that really captured me. It must have been the way he directly addressed readers that struck me. His fiction was of course not normal, not linear. It was as if he were sitting with you and talking to you, but in the voice of some kooky grandfather. I never thought of it like that before, but it was like listening to an older person who knew something and didn't mind sharing it with you if you would listen.

I was never turned off by the drug addiction, homosexuality, graphic violence, language, or sex that occurs in most of his work. I have heard objections to this content on the basis of immorality or prurient interest, and I have heard praise of the same content as "cool." I don't agree with either of these assessments. I believe despite any faults that he had in his personal life or as a person in general, William S. Burroughs was a great moralist unlike any other I have ever encountered. The message that comes through again and again in his work is that there is so much indecency in the so-called straight world. I have not yet encountered another writer who so vehemently is against that without saying it directly or preaching about it. Burroughs demonstrated it.

In that sense, I don't feel that his work is either immoral or cool. I simply think that he was a fringe member of society at best and he used the stuff about which he knew as the basis of his observations. That is what writers do.

In my own life, around the same time I learned to read my first books, I managed to draw the scorn of a large group of boys at my school. My school was divided into two, and one class was advanced learning and the other was "regular" learning. I was advanced. The regular kids were tough and mean in my eyes and they made sure to demonstrate to those around us that they were tougher and meaner than we were.

I don't know why I drew their scorn; that is, I don't remember what happened. By the time I was beneath their gaze, I was too scared to think. It was suggested to me much later that I may have said something or projected something to make them angry, and I still to this day do not know if that was the case or not. It is not what I remember.

I remember that the leader of this gang was tall and muscular. I was not. I remember that he had no trouble looking me in the eyes and talking to me in any way that he wanted. I could not. I do remember that he always had someone backing him up; they would often stand to the side and behind him with just as mean faces, and add appropriate insults at the right time. I do not remember who stood behind me and if they said anything or not.

My basic trick was survival was to avoid confrontation. I can remember my brother who had boxed telling me to stand up to them, but there was simply no way I could summon the courage or even imagine how to do this. I wanted to, of course, and I hated the leader, and all of them, but that was a dream.

I looked away, walked away, stayed away, ran away; in short, I did anything never to fight these guys. They had me beat, there was nothing I could ever do about it, and that was the way it was and always was going to be period.

I had to get creative in my avoidances. Sometimes I would stay in during recess if I felt the heat was too strong. Other times I would play behind remote buildings. I started leaving class as soon as possible at the end of the day, and I had one friend that lived close enough to the school who agreed to let me hide in his house long enough for the fuss to pass. I found alternate ways of getting home.

It wasn't that bad. I guess most of the time I got along, and most of the people in my advanced class got along with me well enough, but as every kid who has ever been picked on knows, you never know when the bullies are going to get restless and come looking. And always, always, always, beware of sports and playgrounds or any situation where you are alone.

I remember one time in particular when things were bad, I took the back way home. The guys were mad at me for some more than ordinary reason and the leader M---- called me out and announced that this day for sure he was kicking my ass after school even if he had to follow me all the way home. Naturally, I didn't want this to happen, so in addition to my schoolwork, I spent the day plotting my escape.

After school I ducked out and started home by the safe way. I cleared the school and was on my way so that I felt pretty good. I ran for insurance and when I got near my street I hid in a bush for double insurance. I waited awhile, long enough so that I was sure they had given up. When I finally crawled out, I started home.

As I rounded my street corner, I witnessed a group of what looked like ten guys walking up the street from my house toward me. Jack was at the lead, the pack was big, and I noticed that guys from the regular pack that didn't even pick on me were with him. I guess they didn't want to miss the show. I immediately and with prejudice ran back the way I came. I wasn't exceptionally fast, but I sprinted down the street behind mine, in case they had seen me, snuck into my neighbor's backyard and hopped the fence into mine. I grabbed the hidden key and let myself in. Disaster avoided.

That night my family and I probably ate dinner as usual. I never told anybody about my troubles. As far as I was concerned, this was the way life was supposed to be. There was no such thing as help.

It wasn't so bad. My friends who knew of these troubles didn't judge me as far as I could tell. The rest of the advanced kids didn't say anything. The regular kids got along and nobody messed with them.

It wasn't so bad. Neither M---- nor any of the guys ever once punched me. They might have pushed me, belittled me, emasculated me in front of every boy and girl at school, called me whatever they wanted, but they didn't kill me. It wasn't so bad.

It wasn't that bad. By the time I moved into other grades, I was well-trained in how to avoid fights so that every time I got into a scuffle with another kid, they won. People generally like when they win, so if you bitchify yourself, they won't kill you. It's not so bad.

You might've guessed that all this depressed me for awhile, and if you did, you're right. *It wasn't so bad.* I lived.

I think about twenty years after the M---- et al experience, a better taught me to reframe it as a *survival* story. That helped.

It wasn't so bad.

I don't tell you this for your sympathy. I am a white male, early 30's, handsome, decent shape, intelligent, middle class. I am of western European descent. I am the benefit of a system which itself benefited from years of exploiting others. I understand. It's not so bad.

My parents, despite any faults they may have had, faithfully and habitually put food in my belly, a roof over my head, and discipline in my mind for education. They helped me a lot.

A lot of people helped me. Mostly, they helped me by telling me things. I learned by listening.

No, I don't tell you any of this for sympathy. I don't tell you any of this even for empathy. You will see me and tell yourself that despite whatever you may know I am a spoiled fucker who doesn't deserve anything.

The reason I talk to you is because there is really no way for you to take away anything from me unless you listen to me. My visual projection is of no consequence to anyone. You have to listen to me to dig me. Dig?

The story speaks for itself. It is the words of an auditory writer.

[They (people) put in my rightful place based on the form of my flesh and not the content of my character.]

The final word is, "There is no way to know anyone completely through sight alone."

Michael Avery
Oakland, CA
May 2007

MINORITY
SCHIZOPHRENIC

Overture

Game over. You and I or we have lost or won. Everything has always already happened.

I am gone. It was over before it began. I am telling us what happened.

I listened to voices. My voice. His voice. Her voice. Your voice.

"You are a loser."

"You should do this. You should do that."

"Vile filth."

I talked back.

You don't know who's talking.

I don't know who's talking.

I don't know who I am.

I don't know who I is.

Adriana

The ultrasound was wrong.

No. That's not accurate.

The ultrasound was what it was. The doctors and my parents agreed that I was to be a girl. My mother named me Adriana and watched her belly grow. As it did, she grew happier and happier with thoughts of her baby daughter, and my father often put his hands on her stomach to feel my kicking. My older brother anticipated his baby sister.

But when I came out, I had a dick. You should have seen the looks on their faces – I'd describe them but how can I remember? – the doctors embarrassed at their own inability to interpret their technology and my mother desperately disappointed that she would never have a baby girl of her own.

To make up for it, I guess, they let me live in a closet. They called me Adriana. I wore a lacy white skirt with a blue blouse and pink embroidery. I perpetually lived in the closet and never left.

My parents and siblings would come in and out at will. They always smiled and acted happy when they came in. They called it tea time, and when I inquired as to the outside world, they said that it wasn't important and *wasn't life inside the closet so much better?* "I guess so," I said, and if I moped they would say, "It's time for us to leave because you need to be by yourself now."

I didn't know any fucking better. They told me I was a girl despite the millimeter-peter in my loins.

When I turned 18, my father opened the door, gave me a pair of pants and a smoky, charcoal grey sweater with holes in it, and told me to put them on; he said that my name was Adrian Francis Farmer, that I had always been a boy and always would be, and kicked me out the door of the house by way of boot to butt and said with a smile on his face and an arm around my mother, "Have a nice life! Don't come back now, ya hear?" and slammed the door to do what he had always done outside of the closet for 18 years of which I never had any knowledge. Interestingly, my most memorable recollection of that entire day is not a picture at all – it is not my parents standing on the porch waving, nor the color of their house which was, and still is, an awful puke lime green, nor the neighbors who were surprised to see me – my strongest recollection is a feeling of cold. It was snowing and there was virgin white all around and I was cold. Despite the darkness and isolation, the closet was kept warm, but outside of the house was bitter cold and colder still when my parents retreated to their living room and shut the door and the neighbors barred their windows too and I looked up to snow falling from the sky.

I learned later that day was the coldest day in 20 years in our town. It said so in The Farmer's Almanac (no relation).

So I am sitting in my bed at God knows what time in the morning in a very cold sweat remembering all this as I just had a dream. In the dream I was lying on dirt as a knight on a stallion was riding over me. I woke up yelling, and for some reason, thinking of the closet.

12 December 2006

12 December 2006 and they came to my house and ripped me out of bed. It was the shock of soldiers in black with shiny helmets and night-vision goggles and semi-automatics slung over their shoulders that I later remembered. "Where is it? Where is it? Is there anybody else in the house?" What in the hell were they talking about? The lead man spun me around and used his arm to shove me into the wall. My pajama bottoms were pulled down and ripped from my body. My shirt the same. I felt the cold walls of the house whose temperature I always turned down at night to save energy. He patted down my whole body. He shoved some kind of prod up my ass.

Meanwhile, other soldiers ransacked my home. My closets were cleaned. Mattresses and pillows cut with knives. Foam and feathers floated in the air. The whole bit. The noise was hostile and aggressive. I wondered where my dog Spot was.

I heard a chopper outside and lights shone back and forth across the windows. Everything got louder, and it felt like my house was filling up for a convention. I turned my head back to see what exactly everyone was doing when the lead man jammed the butt of his weapon in my neck.

"Uh, uh, fucker. You stay right where I have you."

I thought, *They've turned my apartment upside down looking for...what?*

I never found out for sure, but when they'd found or not found what they were looking for, they took me downtown.

I was completely in their hands then. I later remembered that my life as I had known it was over. I was cold, sitting alone on a bench, wearing another set of pajamas that they allowed me to put on before leaving home. My bare feet stuck to the frozen floor. They had removed my shoes upon entering the station.

The helmeted officers went about their business as if I wasn't there, and they continued wearing their goggles inside, even with the lights on. Occasionally, one of them looked up from his desk and flashed me his teeth. He smiled, but his eyes appeared to laugh. He said, "We got you, fucker. What you gonna do now?"

Torture – Prison

--BEGIN TRANSMISSION--
The first thing they did to me was torture. Plain old simple torture. They beat me up. Dig? They sat me in a chair and punched me in the face. The chair fell backwards and I passed out. I had never taken a solid to the face before.

I came to, and was upright again in the chair. My jaw hurt and I could taste the blood salt on my lips. My sparring partner was staring at me with one hand on my shoulder. He said, "You gotta stay awake now, OK chief?" I could barely make out his silhouette with the lights in my face.

So he went to work on my body. He wised up and put me against a wall so I couldn't fall over anymore. He even had a couple of heavies with urban camouflage on my right and left to prevent my toppling sideways.

He took shot after shot to my gut and then to my face now and again. Just for good measure, I suppose. I could see his form. This was no slouch. Somebody had taught him how to fight at one point. He stood in front of me like a boxer. I couldn't understand why he kept his guard up.

He kept his two dukes up in front of his mouth and rocked back and forth on his feet. He jabbed with his left a couple times and then leaned forward with a hard right. Then he started in with the combos – jab, jab, uppercut, uppercut. Bob and weave. This guy was pro.

He didn't ask any questions for awhile. He just hit me. I kept my mouth shut, but eventually I couldn't take anymore and my head just slumped forward and the blood spilled into my lap. The guy on my left pulled my head back by my hair, but I was gone. My eyes closed.

I woke up in an infirmary strapped to a bed. There was no way to get up. Doctors would come in and out once in a while. I convalesced for an indeterminate amount of time. I was in and out, in and out, always waking in a dream-like fog, blurry-eyed; men in white would come over, administer injections, and I would fade. After awhile, the track marks on my arms began to scab. It was then that the men in white applied rubbing alcohol and I would strain to sit bolt upright except I couldn't because I was strapped down. I tried to scream but some kind of leather strap around my face prevented that, too.

More injections. Sometimes I heard them talk. I couldn't see anymore. I couldn't tell if whether what I was seeing was a dream vision or reality. I stopped trying to tell the difference, or caring. "He's a lucky one," they would say. More injections. And then hyena laughs. I threw up and had to have hoses from mouth to stomach. I had long forgotten about food, but I hallucinated that they had some I.V. or other automatic system keeping me alive. It all really didn't matter.

The doctors stopped showing up. I awoke and assumed I wasn't dreaming. I enjoyed the fact that the injections stopped and the track marks began to heal for good even without rubbing alcohol. I could see out of my peripheries that there were other beds with other bodies, but they didn't move and I couldn't have communicated with them anyway, nor they with me, I assumed. The entire set up was white white white. Everywhere white. Unnervingly so. I played it cool and chilled.

After the infirmary a large man in black threw me into the general population. Some kind of a yard with many dudes. There was an entire social order revolving around male body size. Big guys with bald heads and massive arms, chests, legs, and necks stood still like stars while guys of smaller proportions gravitated and revolved around them like planets.

I was a small guy at 5'4". I observed.

Every day at 2 o'clock the large man in black pulled me into a small office with a table in the middle and doors on either side. I entered one door, took a seat, and waited. After a short time, a thin man in a white coat would enter through the opposite door. He sat and asked me questions. "Did you steal the plans? What did you do with the plans?"

"I'm not sure what you are talking about." I always told the truth, but he never seemed to believe me.

He'd redirect and start asking about the yard or telling me about his wife, and after I laughed at some joke of his, he'd stand up straight and stare me down and say, "So tell me what you did with those plans."

"Really, I don't know what you're talking about."

He would push a button and the large man in black re-entered with a couple of armed guards, also in jet black. They each sidled up on either side of me and leveled their automatic weapons to my temples. The thin man in white would lean over the table and smile nice and thick with bad breath and say, "Now take it easy and you won't get hurt." He would proceed to inject me with some translucent liquids. The guards lowered their weapons and left after he finished the procedure. Then the doctor would continue asking about the yard or telling me about his wife. About 15 minutes later, I got dizzy and passed out and woke up back in general population.

I started acting erratically. I never wanted to sit still. Strangely, I held my tongue around others. I wanted to talk but only allowed myself to talk aloud when I was alone. I tried to maintain by keeping strictly to myself. My mind began drawing connecting lines between everything it saw. I saw a guy in the yard and thought of the doctor who in turn reminded me of a man I knew sometime before any of this had happened. I believed that they all knew each other. I couldn't recall names.

People began to blur together until I wasn't sure who I was talking with. I said to the doctor, "Quit fucking me in the showers," and I told the guy who was fucking me in the showers that I didn't know what plans he wanted. My idea about keeping to myself stopped working, and guys in the yard started complaining. Even the guys who bitch-fucked me said, "Man, you *are* a little queer." I started doing numerical calculations in my free time and reasoned that I had been in this facility for three months. All of my observations and calculations were based on intuition.

The thin man in white from my daily meetings finally said to me, "Number 28, we are going to have to put you in isolation for awhile. Some of the men in the yard are having a hard time dealing with you. There have been complaints." He pushed the button and the large man in black entered to lead me away.

"Oh, I almost forgot," the thin man said. "Don't forget to take these every day. It should help…with things." He smiled big and handed me a 2 quart container which was split into 7 sections. Each section contained a colorful array of what looked like Halloween candy. Colored pills like Sweet-Tarts. Different sizes, different doses.

Things changed. I lived in solitary confinement. Someone left food and water and pills…everyday? hour? There was a hole to shit in, and a blanket to cover me at night. The floor was cement and the paint job on the walls was peeling. My feet slapped the floor. I had no slippers. Sometimes they left the lights on for…days? weeks? Just to screw with my sense of time, I suppose. And other times I lived in relative darkness for periods. When I told the guard who slipped me my food and water that I was sorry and would do *anything* for regular hours, they moderated the light and dark in what felt like consistent intervals.

Time passed. I lost track of how much. My intuition, with nothing to refer to, began to fail. My room, a closet really, was completely white. It couldn't have been more than 10' x 10' x 10'.

I often paced to stay warm or pass time. When the lights were out, I had to be careful not to fall into the shitter.

This was it. They knew that each passing day, each passing hour now, I was breaking down. They were giving me food and water, but I began refusing to eat. I began to see the bones under my skin. My mind continued to race.

I raced. Sometimes I would run in place for…minutes? hours? I thought I was getting somewhere. I thought I was going to get out and emerge a better person. I didn't know how I got here, why I was here, where here was, who these people were, what was going to happen, or when I was going to get out; but it had to be good. I believed it so.

My teeth started falling out.

But escape wasn't their idea. I was not going anywhere. They were waiting to see. Waiting to see what I would do.

They wanted to see a human act like an electron and bounce off the walls of his atom-cell until his head caved in.

--END TRANSMISSION--

Inscrutable Pete

I'm so damn tired of everybody telling me that I don't put enough feelings into my work. I'm a writer. I write. I write stories about things that happened to me, and the most frequent comment I hear is, "You don't explain why your character is doing what he's doing. We don't know his thoughts or feelings." My question back is, "Why should my character be obligated to tell his thoughts and feelings?"

All my life people have been telling me, "Pete, you are too nice a guy. You wear your heart on your sleeve." They are trying to warn me of not being too vulnerable lest

I get taken advantage of by less scrupulous types. For years, I didn't know what they meant.

How ironic that now, the guy whose school voted him Most-Likely-To-Be-Nice, should be accused of stubborn obstinance.

How dare they. How fucking dare they. Don't they know who they are fucking with?

I was crying with a broken heart when they were still somewhere between the womb and the grave. I was here before they were. I was crushed again and again for trusting every Tom Dick and Harry that walked up or down the street. I saw 100 Jills ride off with 100 Jacks 100 times before they even had a first date. I died 100 times.

When it was worst, the best anybody ever told me was that I would have to take care of myself. "Nobody is going to do it for you," they said. Funny thing to be starving at a 10 course meal at a table full of guests laughing and carrying on, not knowing what hands are for, and seeing the faces of the others laughing but not offering so much as a crumb of bread. What were they thinking? I couldn't tell you, for Inscrutable Pete was never in that position.

So Inscrutable Pete learned that no matter what the fuck is the matter, nobody is going to lend a hand. The philosophy is simple – "Anyone not capable of taking care of himself is one less idiot that I have to worry about."

Hands are for taking. Even if you are stupid, you eventually suss out that everybody's M.O. is to take as much as they can all the time while giving up the least amount of whatever, all the time.

Inscrutable Pete learned that hands are for taking, returned to the dinner party, and started gobbling up a plateful. Boy was he hungry. It was a little awkward for everybody at first. I.P. eating like he'd never tasted food before and the guests just sitting there, flabbergasted, their laughs suddenly silenced. I.P. looked up from his turkey and cranberry sauce and paused, "What?" They didn't say a word, and then the silence was so thick you could eat it.

"Well, what the fuck?" he said. "Did you think I *died*?"

What is my problem? I'll tell you what my problem is. My problem is them. Who the fuck do they think they are? What do they know that's so fuckin' special?

If Inscrutable Pete tells you that one day he picked up a fuckin' backpack and humped it from Reno, Nevada to the Badlands, North Dakota, and met Dr. Sees-in-the-Dark, and sat with him at the campfire until Dr. pulled out a leaf and said, "Put that in your pipe and smoke it," and did until Pete the Inscrutable saw himself atop a great plateau looking down at the broken hoop blah blah blah, what's it to them?

Why did I do it? Fuck you.

Kurt Vonnegut said something along the lines of, "You have to give the reader the experience of a great date; otherwise, the reader is liable to get bored and leave at any minute. Readers are under no *obligation* to be decent whatsoever" (emphasis added).

Inscrutable Pete is tired of giving away his good experiences to insensitive readers who are simply selfish and want a good time at his expense. He has spent much time catering to their every need, and he is tired. "We want to understand," they tell him, and then goose him as he prepares to deliver.

Kurt V. realized that people are basically mean, selfish animals who use.

Inscrutable Pete agrees.

Can you smell what Inscrutable Pete is cookin'?

Who you waiting for?

Prince Charming is dead. He died 1000 times for you. The first time he came to town he was young with a smile on his face, clean teeth, smooth skin, and long straight blonde hair. His snow-white steed Rusty pranced. The Prince confronted the Duke who stared him down with a 12-inch advantage. The Duke crushed PC's nuts with one massive squeeze of his extra large iron gauntlet and cut off his legs at the knees. The Duke unrolled his hose, stroked it up real good, and face fucked him in front of Rusty and the local villagers. After he finished, he used toothpicks to hold open the Prince's eyelids, told him to beg for mommy, and cut his head clean-off in a single stroke with a two-handed broad sword the way a major league slugger sends a hard ball over the center field wall 400 feet out.

The Prince came again with a smile on his face and clean, well-brushed, white teeth. This time the Duke made him kiss the floor while keeping his butt up in the air. The Duke whispered to Rusty who whinnied and mounted his master. After the Prince was all out of tears but bleeding from the anus, the Duke bit his dick off and fed it to the dogs. The Duke then cut off his legs and arms, nicknamed him Art – but didn't bother hanging him on a wall – and planted him in a garden instead.

The Prince came again with a smile and clean pearly white teeth, but this time the Duke let him into the Keep. The Duke gave him a prostitute who the Prince thought was the Princess. The prostitute gave him syphilis and gonorrhea, and after he discovered his diagnosis, the Duke gave him to the henchmen who were tired of the prostitute themselves and who proceeded to gangfuck PC until he was bleeding from every hole. Then they scalped him and took him to the woods. Nobody saw him again, and the men came back laughing.

The Prince came back again, and this time the Duke armed the villagers with rifles for sport and they picked him and Rusty off from a distance until they both lay in a pool of blood and mud. The villagers each unloaded another 500 rounds into their unrecognizable corpses, just for good measure.

The Prince came again and faced the Duke in the square. PC held his chin high and proud, but the Duke put a sawed off shotgun in his mouth, agreed to let him go if he would fellate the shaft for five minutes, changed his mind, and left him with the finishing surprise instead.

The Prince came again and the Duke shoved a pike up his cornhole.

The Prince came again and the Duke unloaded a full magazine of ammunition from an automatic machine gun with a high powered scope at point blank into the PC's face.

The Prince came again and was tied down to Rusty who was made to step into blocks of wet cement. After the blocks dried, PC and Rusty were thrown into the moat and eaten by piranhas.

The Prince came again and was drawn and quartered. His heart was pulled out still beating and forced fed to him.

The Prince came again and was forced at gunpoint to sauté his own testicles in garlic butter and made to eat them after which he was shot in the head.

The Prince came again and was ground up through a sausage grinder and fed to the villagers for every major holiday, both religious and government, so nobody would feel left out.

The Prince came again and was sodomized with steel strap-ons by the duchy prostitutes.

The Prince came again and was hanged from the gallows with razor wire. Instead of breaking his neck, the wire popped his head like a wine cork and his body fell limp to the ground.

The Prince came again. And again. And again. Etc. He had understood that the Princess was in the tower. He only ever met the Duke.

PC thought the Duke was the King and never realized that the Duke's lady was the Duchess and not the Princess. PC learned the hard way.

Don't you know that Prince Charming is the Duke's bitch?

Prince Charming is dead.

Who you waiting for?

You Shouldn't Be Here

Jan'07:Dear Diary,

What's everyone up to?

Like barging into your mother and father having sex.

"You shouldn't be here. GET OUT OF HERE!"

Your father explaining to you that you don't belong in here: "It's mommy and daddy's room. When the door is closed, you have to knock."

There are rules, rules we learn, rules we follow.

They won't be written down. They won't be spoken in public.

But they will be understood.

And if we don't?

Well, then, God help us.

You shouldn't be here.

O Mama, Where Art Thou?

Cocks, balls and assholes. That's all it's been so far.

Notice I don't mention vaginas.

In a pinch, any orifice will do. Even some straight men want to put it up an ass, and many have successfully convinced their partners to do so thereby avoiding any accusations of being gay.

Recollect Dan Savage: I'm not trying to tell straight men not to think about their penises. I'm trying to tell straight men *to think about vaginas.*

I would consider myself lucky to have somebody to hug and love and lie in bed with at night under warm covers.

The mountaintop is great if you want to see, but you learn right quick that the wind bites up there and it's no place to live. A horrible feeling is being 13,000 feet off the ground on your way toward space and the closest thing you have left to a warm body is a memory so far removed you'd rather not remember.

I, Tiresias

I, Tiresias, both man and woman, blind yet sighted, exist again. I have arrived here not by my own choosing, yet I find myself here nonetheless. How many appearances this makes for me I do not know, but as before, I am generally regarded as an oddity and, therefore, shunned.

I, Tiresias, who was man, then woman, am man again. Who understands me? Who recognizes me?

I was asked[1] by Zeus, my lord, "Who feels more pleasure during copulation, man or woman?" Hera, his lady, stood next to him and Zeus, by Jove, demanded I answer. Fearing his wrath, I dared not refuse, and owing to my reputation, could not say but the truth.

"For every 1/10 pleasure a man feels, 9/10 more a woman receives." And Hera his lady did declare herself superior so that Zeus changed me from man to woman for my answer.

"You will experience the superiority of woman," he said. And I wandered then, as Tiresias, the woman.

From woman back to man I became by various ways, until I was Tiresias that I had been.

I am Tiresias, the man who was woman.

Woman

I feel like a woman. I feel like I have taken it up the ass a few times. Once would have been too much.

In a closed environment containing only males, when one man forces his piece on another, the another is called a "bitch". That is, bitch derived from the female version of canine, metaphorically referring to the female version of the human species.

I feel feminized and emasculated.

Wolves to the left of me, bulls to the right, here I am, stuck in the middle – sittin' bitch.

---

[1] "Tiresias," *Wikipedia.* 12 December 2006. My account of this myth was fictionalized from the Wikipedia article.

They Are Coming

"The last time I checked, if someone puts a gun to your head and pulls the trigger, that's homicide." I looked with dead seriousness at my friend who had asked me a question.

Friend. Wouldn't call him that exactly. He was the person with whom I was currently associating. I didn't trust him. I learned a long time ago not to trust anybody. That sounds paranoid, I know, but it's not so bad once you get used to it.

"Yes, but don't you think if you continue doing what you're doing, you're going to get yourself killed?"

"I don't know."

"I'd be careful if I were you."

There. He betrayed himself. Even he could see that the trajectory of my life was leading me to a place where some people would want me dead.

His original question was, "What? Are you suicidal?"

Maybe I was. Maybe he was right. I had been doing research at local libraries on schizophrenia. I gained knowledge of certain things in the medical community that were less than forthright, if you know what I mean, and when I began to speak publicly about my findings, I began to feel the heat. I heard footsteps behind me at night. I noticed shadows in blind alleys.

I met my friend with whom I was currently associating at the library. He was part of the literacy program in our town, and we met in the stacks. I told him what I was up to, and he seemed interested.

We started hanging out, but now he was saying I was going too far. He was criticizing me, telling me, "No Adrian, don't do that; it's suicide."

Maybe he was right, but as I told him, "The last time I checked, if someone puts a gun to your head and pulls the trigger, that's homicide."

We were sitting on the steps of the water fountain at the square of the city. It was lunch time, and all the workers were out enjoying their food. The sun was out, but it was chilly on this late fall day.

"We live in the United States of America," I told him. "We have freedom of speech."

"Yes, but there are other laws at work here. For instance, if you rock the boat, the Captain is going to get mad. If the Captain gets mad, you've got a problem."

Of course, he was right. But that didn't concern me. I felt compelled to tell the truth.

I pressed on in my quest both to uncover the truth about schizophrenia and to spread it. Several attempts on my life were made and failed each time. I came very close to dying on several occasions. The last time was the scariest. I told my wife to pour my hot water for oatmeal and that I was just going to get the paper. I opened the door and walked out into the crisp morning and bright daylight. I grabbed the gazette which lay on my door mat. The headline read: "They are coming. They will find you. They pry. Best hide. It is an unlucky soul who finds itself in the camera eye. 'Anonymity is a virtue…'" I shook my head, puzzled, and suddenly felt two bullets whiz past my face and shatter the window next to the door. I ran inside, slammed the door, told my wife to call the police, and waited for help to arrive.

"How did you get here?" – A Dream

The judge asks the question. There is no jury. It's simply he facing me, with the world behind.

"Of course that's a loaded question, your Honor. Allow me to explain myself.

"That question works on so many levels I can't begin to answer it without going into some detail. First of all, there is the obvious, how did I get here – meaning, how I arrived at this courthouse, today. The answer to that would be that I was brought here, by the police, from the jail. But I think I can safely assume that is not the answer you are looking for."

He doesn't smile at me.

"So, before I can attempt to answer the question beyond that, I must first ask a question of my own. What do you mean by that?"

"What I mean, and what I think the audience is interested in, is how did you come to assume your position in life?"

"Please clarify."

"Simply put, we are in a situation here where you have been declared a lunatic. You have earned the disgust of the audience. They desire, I may venture, to see you institutionalized. What we would like to know before we relieve you of your…well, let's just say, before we continue further…what we would like to know is how did you manage to get yourself into this position? How did you manage you draw the disgust of us all?"

I look over my shoulder at the crowd. I think I hear the sharpening of metal on whetstones, and I see glistening steel in the hands of audience members ready to vault the bar; but seeing my eyes, and looking at the judge, they hold their positions.

I look forward again at the judge and now he begins to smirk.

I lose my place. I grow confused. I forget what I am going to say and feel panic shoot up through my spine and out my neck. My hairs stand on end.

I want to faint but can't. My legs are solid.
I choke up.
"I don't know, your Honor."

Who was I talking to?

I was talking to myself for years. Who was listening?
What does it mean, "to talk to myself?" It means to speak
aloud when no one is in the room with me.

A psychologist once told me, "It's no problem if
you talk to yourself. Some people think out loud." A
writer once said, "You don't have to worry about talking to
yourself; it's when you begin answering yourself that you
should worry." Or did he say, "When you start hearing
voices?"

Worry be damned. Suppose for a moment you do
talk to yourself, how do you do it?

Let's say you are getting ready for a big speech in
front of 10,000 people and you are trying to relax yourself.
You're doing the old pep talk shtick. Do you say, "I need
to calm down. I need to breathe. I need to relax and not
worry about this so much. It's a piece of cake." Or do you
say, "Calm down. Breathe. Relax and don't worry so
much. This is a piece of cake."

Take it from this wigger – I have tried it both ways.
I don't remember which way I started, but the day I
switched gave me a funny sensation. I mean, let's say I'm
for years doing it way number two. I am telling myself
what to do. "Do this. Do that. Jump up. Sit down. Keep
your mouth shut. Spill your guts. Beat off. Take a shit.
Run down a fucking street naked while screaming at the top
of your fucking lungs." Then one day I hear the voice – I
mean *hear* the voice, apart from myself – and switch. I
shift the subject from "you," the second person, to "I," the

first person. "*I* need to sit down. *I* need to keep my mouth shut. *I* need to spill my guts. *I* need to beat off. *I* need to take a shit. *I* need to run down a fucking street naked while screaming at the top of my fucking lungs."

Really? (voice of Jim Carrey as Ace Ventura)

Interesting. (voice of the author)

Sounds a little weird, huh? I mean, who really talks to him or herself like that? I mean, who really talks to him or herself in the first person?

But this wigger tried it. Sure it sounds a little funny, but what the fuck? I am for years doing the latter, way number two, and now I am doing the former, way number one. I have switched the subject from second person to first person.

But being schizophrenic and inclined to an overactive brain, I start to ask questions: *Who in the fuck has been telling me to do all this shit over the years? Who is this fucking voice in my head? Where does it come from?*

I recollected the voices I heard and began to suss out that things I'd heard people say were actually coming through my head. I was, in the past, in a full-tilt boogie by myself and suddenly stopped and realized that I was mouthing the words of some dumbshit I heard 10 years prior.

Furthermore, I dug that if I was talking to myself in the second person, then how could I have been the subject and the object of the sentence at the same time? I mean, if I was all, "Calm down man. Take a chill pill," then how could I have been the "you" talking to the "man" listening at the same time? At least had I accepted the lame sounding "I need to be calm; I need to take a chill pill," then I would have been *I* and there would have been no *you* and we would not have needed to discuss to whom I was talking.

But who the fuck talks to him or herself like that? I mean, in the first person?

I know it all sounds academic and could be explained how within certain contexts it all makes perfect sense; but after one has been in prison and administered a never-ending cocktail, one begins to wonder. And hearing that voice even after he stops talking aloud…well, you catch my drift.

Check this. You ever had it like this? Let's say you just got into an argument with a friend, and you realize your friend tricked you and got away with some shit by which you are now appalled. You have been deceived and you are trying to muster the wherewithal to keep going. You say to yourself, "Don't ever let them do that to me again. Never let 'em say that shit to me."

You, them, me. What the fuck is going on here?

Anyway, come to realize, it don't fucking matter, man. The only thing all this thinking means is that this wigger is fucked up.

Subject? Object? I am the one with the fucking diagnosis.

"You shouldn't know that"

I looked at the older guy with sudden suspicion and he eyed me coldly. What he was referring to, of course, was the statement I had just made. I had told him with confidence that the trick to mastering any activity which involves doing two things simultaneously such as rubbing your tummy and patting your head is to slow it down to the point that you can actually do it. After that, you can speed it up with relative ease to however fast you want.

"You shouldn't know that," is how he responded.

I can't take credit for that piece of wisdom. I read it in a book. Gordon Sumner said it. He was referring to his ability to play a song like "When the World Is Running Down, You Make the Best of What's Still Around" and sing at the same time. If you listen to that song, you will hear that his bass line is quite syncopated in relation to the melody line and, in fact, the other instruments in the song. So, he said, the trick is slowing it down. If you can master that, then it's just a matter of speeding up. Which is easy.

So I tried it for myself. I did exactly what he said. Of course, he was right.

I rubbed my tummy slow enough so that I could pat my head at the same time. Getting it to work felt like I was breaking my arms.

The older guy watched me demonstrate. He scowled and demonstrated how well he could do it at three times the speed of me.

I shut my mouth.

"Still," he said. "You shouldn't know that."

Schizomania

Run don't walk. Slow down. Lightning synapse explodes electricity faster than speed of sound but not quite speed of light. Chemical slow down. The manic brain doesn't sleep. Better get some rest. Go for a jog. Meditate. Do some pushups. Watch TV.

Stop!

Restart

Fuck run don't walk. To really make time, you gotta drive don't run. Fly don't drive. Steal an F-16 Tomcat don't take passenger air. Teleport don't fly. Just be there anyway you can anytime anyhow now.

You are already there.

Dig?

Technique

Now that we have that out of the way…the technique is simple. Start with sound. The sound speeds up synapses which fire faster and faster upon invisible lines of association. You travel.

So you find yourself a sauna somewhere. The kind that gets real hot. You gotta sweat. Get music piped in over a loudspeaker, but music that you can control with a handheld device. You are sitting in the sauna sweating listening to that which gets you off. "Ladies and gentlemen we are now floating in space."

"Eruption." Alex starts with a drum roll like the firing of a V-8 engine and Eddie follows with a piston pounding guitar solo. "Eruption" literally is one. 14 January 2007 and you are time traveling to Los Angeles circa 1977. "Eruption" occurred nearly thirty years prior, but it feels like it's going to shoot right up through your ass into mid-air. The notes make your hair stand on end even in the sauna. You cannot believe that a body could actually do that.

Now it doesn't matter if you don't reference Van Halen – two Dutch Los Angelenos. Substitute Jimi Hendrix, Pete Townsend, Jimmy Page, B.B.King, Charlie

Christian, or Andres friggin' Segovia – so long as it gets you off.

Now your brain is running. You are making connections at the speed of…sound? Approximately 796 mph. You don't worry about writing anything down. No time at this speed, and any kind of writing implement – be it pad and pen or pencil or typewriter or word processor – would be a major hassle in this environment. You are going to have to trust your memory. Just lay back and listen and enjoy the Good Fix. You can repeat to yourself a few good ideas that trickle up from wherever for later investigation. This is the technique.

Skip around. Load up all your favorites. Try jazz rock swing. Try classical punk death-metal. Try pop torch songs Broadway show tunes. Try fast slow fast. It doesn't matter. Your only responsibility is to please yourself. It has to get you off. If you don't enjoy it, you miss the boat.

As you shower and towel off, calm down and focus on slow things. The floor, the condensed steam dripping down the egg shell tile wall, the dirty brown potato you're going to bake for dinner.

> Note: training school cannot
> quite prepare you for
> the come down after
> breaking the sound
> barrier. *Queasiness is
> a standard byproduct.*

You Are Objectifiable

"I" is an alien from outer space. "I" inhabits the proper name Adrian Francis Farmer that has attached itself to a human body. Who is "I"? "I" is simply subject. Subject is ego by definition. The body known to other humans as

Adrian Francis Farmer is not subject. Adrian Francis Farmer is empty vessel. Adrian Francis Farmer is subject or object or both to varying degrees at any given moment in any given coordinates. Divorce "I" and discover that what you understand is you is not you. You don't know yourself.

Panic in the streets. General hysteria. What we can expect from populations who are largely uninformed and confused by this interpretation.

Who is "you?"

Analysis of preceding phrase reveals that word "you" is made third person by "incorrect" use of verb "is".

"You" is objectifiable.

You are objectifiable.

Duality. Binary. Subject/object. Good/evil. Up/down. Right/left. Etc. World as experienced by humans trapped in duality. Outcome uncertain. Transcend duality. How? Accept that which we cannot understand.

Lay down your weapons and come out with your hands down.

Faith is everything will work out one way or another.

This as far we go.

Goodbye.

Documentation for Writing Style

Changing the grammar for simple structures such as "I am" to "I is" effectively treats words as symbols instead of concepts. "I" as a symbol is generally accepted to represent the self or the ego. But an investigation of language should reveal that it has nothing to do with our selves. "We" is not ourselves.

Therefore, treating language as a symbolic system without fixed meaning illustrates its objectivity.

Many people can't seem to separate their identities from the language they use. They simply can't see that the utterance "I am tall" has nothing to do with who they are as people. This creates confusion. Confusion leads to…violence, hatred, manipulation, deception, etc., whatever.

Drawing attention to language as separate symbolic system apart from actual human beings illustrates clarity.

Clarity trumps correcticity in this game, every time.

Jimi Hendrix

"…arguably the greatest electric guitar player of the 20th century."

"Yeah, but do you know why he played a right-handed guitar?"

My mind drifted. The constant noise of the waves of the ocean reminded me of a mother cradling her baby, and I wanted to lie down to sleep. It was white noise – constant nurturing din. I guess I likened it to a mother's soft lullaby.

We had come here to the lighthouse to visit. We were friends. We met about five years ago.

I liked Bob. He had a likeable knack; a certain ability to disarm even the most stubborn fool. I was a stubborn fool and he was my friend.

"Well, do you?" he repeated.

"Dude, I got one for you." I changed the conversation.

"What?" he asked, playing along in good humor.

"You know why everybody shakes with their right hand?"

"No. Why?"

"Well, they would've gone with the left if it weren't for us 10% weirdoes who are left-handed."

"Ah, shit, you read my mind, man."

I didn't know what he meant, but I kept going. "See, right-handers wipe their asses with their right hands and lefties wipe with their lefts. So 90% of the people are shoving their right hands near their poopers an average of twice a day. It would make sense to have everyone shake with their lefts since you've got a 90% chance of shaking a clean hand. But no, that's not how they figure, see? The right-handers think, 'There is no fucking way I'm gonna let some left-handed punk-ass bitch pass his shit off on me. No way, no how.' So they agree to shake with their rights. So, majority rules, and voila."

"But that doesn't make any sense. You're saying that we decided to shake with our right hands just to spite lefties?"

"That's exactly what I'm saying."

"But then everybody is spreading their shit all over the place!"

"Exactly," I said.

"You gotta weird way of looking at things," he replied.

"See, nobody thinks of it as their shit hand because everyone's been told to wash their hands after they do their business. But we've been in men's rooms, man. We've seen the shit in there. The shit on the ground. The shit and piss all over the seat. The shit on the walls. The walls, man! The walls! We're a bunch of fucking animals!"

Bob just looked at me, but he was clearly enjoying my antics.

I continued. "So, it is a right-handed world, and everyone is *supposed* to wash their hands and nobody is supposed to spread any shit around. Now, do you really believe, after all, that everyone's following the rules? You think everybody's washing their hands?"

His smile stopped short. "Fuck dude," he said.

"Anyway, the truth is: right-handers don't like left-handers. We're the fucking minority and they don't fucking trust us. They'd rather risk taking shit 90% of the time from their own kind than risk taking shit 10% of the time from lefties, simply because if they do it the second way, they can't pass shit back to lefties. Ever."

I paused for effect. "'Fuck the lefties!' We catch their shit 90% of the time and are only lucky once every ten days."

Bob doubled over. "That was funny, man. I never thought of it that way. You ought to be a comedian."

"I guess," I replied.

"But like I was saying before you *steamrolled* me, 'You read my mind.'"

"What do you mean?" I asked.

"Why did Jimi Hendrix play a right-handed guitar?"

I thought back to when I had changed the conversation. "I don't know," I said.

"Cuz that's what he had. It's way easier to find a right-handed guitar than it is to find a left-handed one."

I chuckled. "I think you're right, dude."

"And do you know why he played it left-handed?"

I sensed where this was going, but I listened to the waves crashing below. The lighthouse above was dormant. It had been abandoned a long time ago, its use forgotten. The waves kept feeding-back. I forgot to reply to Bob.

"Cuz that's the hand he beat off with." He chuckled to himself and looked at me. I forgot everything in that moment – who I was, who he was, where we were, etc, etc.

– but I snickered because that was a good one. I kept my eyes on the waves.

Thinking back, he must have felt rejected. "What's up man? You O.K.? I thought you liked my jokes?" he asked.

The waves crashed on the rocks and released great suds of white.

"Yeah, man. I like them. Nothing's wrong."

But I lied. The truth was that I was lost.

I didn't know.

Temple of Robin Hood

The band is Temple of Robin Hood. The song is "Can I Have Some More." The idea for the video is this – as the guitar arpeggio commences to the steady beat of the hi-hat, a Caucasian man sits at the head of the table, alone, and the table is 100 feet long with place settings for as many people. The candelabras are there but not lit, and there is curiously no food either. The man is smiling, all teeth, and the creases in his cheek are longer than an inch. He wears a black suit, long, straight blond hair, and a king's crown on his head, red velvet with gold leafing. At about thirty seconds, Chris, the singer, chimes in: "I don't mind, stealing bread, from the mouths of decadents…"[2] At this point, a decanter lowers into view. It is sterling, shining silver, and metallic without reflection. It tips by the force of a white hand and out comes burgundy wine. The king at the table has his right arm outstretched gripping a goblet. His mouth, teeth, and cheeks never so much as flinch. He is statuesque. Chris continues – "Cuz I can't feed on the powerless, when my cup's already overfilled…" And the

---

[2] Temple of the Dog. "Hungerstrike." *Temple of the Dog.* A&M, 1991. The lyrics of my fictional song are taken from this actual song.

burgundy wine begins to runneth over. By the time the band kicks in, the decanter has been pouring steadily for a minute. One must wonder, Where is all the wine coming from? We can rig a device to feed the decanter with an unlimited supply of gallons. And the wine pours right on through the entire song. Four and a half minutes. The cup runnething over. It is all we need.

Depending on viewer response, we can add in montages of the distended bellies of starving children overlaid on the king for effect. Personally, I find that a little distasteful, but if the audience demands, it can be done.

Propose Space Travel

Call it the Mayflower. Call it the Love Boat. How did Bradford, Standish, and all the rest survive on that frigate, exactly? What kind of system did they have? They left the King behind; so who was running the show?

The Mayflower is a spaceship. It's a moving biosphere. Its purpose is to get the hell off this rock. The reason the Mayflower has come about is because the current movement to get into outer space is not happening fast enough. Sure, Mars can be reached. With current technology 22 January 2007, it might be a 15 year mission. But it is known that there isn't much on Mars except Red Desert. Sure, there might be hidden layers of water and ice which give great support to the idea that life might have been on Mars at one time. There is at least one theory that says Mars was hit by an asteroid.[3] A chunk of it blew into outer space, carrying all the germs it needed to start life, and floated to Earth. Earthlings could be Martians.

---

[3] *Aliens of the Deep*, dir. James Cameron and Steven Quale. Buena Vista Pictures, 2005. The following theory was taken from the movie.

Another theory suggests that life might exist on one of Jupiter's moons. As far as scientists can tell, Europa is a solid block of ice. Theory speculates that if one were to send a rocket propelled drill deep into the core of Europa, one might discover a liquid center with live organisms due to chemo-synthesis. Appears a worthy hypothesis suitable for research to this reporter.

But if human beings are to really get out into space, they have to leave the solar system. Mars and Europa are Earth's immediate neighbors, and if humans want any chance of really getting somewhere, they will have to leave the local community and go explore other parts of the city, i.e. galaxy.

The Mayflower or Love Boat is sponsored. Whether by government or corporation doesn't matter. It will take money to build and assemble the technology. Probably, the governments of Earth are too busy jockeying for control to have a real concerted effort for this type of project. But, it's not the technology that's the problem – it's the system.

The Mayflower has to be totally self-sustaining. Whether the sponsor that builds it can get it to move at 1000 mph or 2000 mph or 20,000 mph, it is going to go slow at best. Recall light travels at approximately 186,000 mps and it takes more than four years for light from Proxima Centauri to reach Earth. The Pilgrims on this new Mayflower will be saying bye to Earth forever.

Inside their boat, the Pilgrims as it were will be completely sustained by the biosphere. They will be able to grow crops, generate oxygen, recycle waste, and maintain the ship itself. They will be able to breed and keep livestock. They will be able to breed and keep themselves.

There will be doctors, scientists, engineers, technicians, teachers, shamans, farmers, writers, painters, sculptors, musicians, actors, athletes – every type of person needed to move away from Earth, keep the boat moving, and set up a new system in a new habitat once it is found. The sponsors will draw these people to itself on the promise of a new life in space. It might take awhile, but if 100 Pilgrims were willing to sail away from known land into unknown water 400 years ago, then it will happen again.

Technology will not be the problem. Humans' best and brightest will find a way to make it work. Always have, always will. The real problem is the system that will have to take place on the Mayflower for the people to get along.

You cannot put 1000 people on the New Mayflower who want to kill each other. They will decimate their entire chances before they reach Pluto. These Pilgrims have to tolerate one another.

Potentially, these Pilgrims can be anybody – and I mean anybody. They would not have to be one race. They could be one of every race on Earth. They could be like Noah's animals. But they could be one race, too. There doesn't even have to be both sexes. On the original Mayflower it was something like 90 men to 10 women, and that was before cloning technology and test tube babies. Nowadays, a entrepreneurial group of females could sponsor the Mayflower, grab all the necessary equipment and DNA material, and start their own civilization with or without males. And vice-versa. It doesn't really matter. What does matter is that everyone onboard the Mayflower agrees to a *common purpose* and is truthful enough about it not to kill everyone else.

Who will sponsor such a mission?

Presidents of wealthy corporations might have enough money to build such ships. Governments, too. However, anybody concerned with maintaining a controlling interest on Earth might find it difficult to spearhead this operation while maintaining control on Earth.

Recollect the original Pilgrims, i.e. Puritans, banded together and took matters into their own hands. They decided for themselves. At any rate, it's back to the issue of system. Once the Mayflower fires up and the bottle is broken on its bow, its crew will never see another Earthling again. It might be 10 generations or more to get to the next star system depending on how fast they can get the hull rattling. Who is going to call the shots?

It doesn't matter.

As long as the Pilgrims onboard agree to the common purpose, it matters not.

What is the common purpose?

To go into space.

Maria

She woke up one winter weekday, not completely herself, and perturbed by a gigantic dagger in her abdomen. How it got there, she did not know, but it ached like the beginnings of a pimple that is felt but not yet seen.

The dagger itself was the most ornate and fashionable blade she had ever seen. Or, more accurately, the handle was the most ornate and fashionable, as the blade was mostly buried within her. The handle was bone, not bleached, but off-white like egg shell, as if it were very old and had been handled many times. At the top of the hilt by the guard, green suede wrapped around the blade in a crossing fashion and it was studded with beveled rubies. She did not bother to count them, although she marveled at their beauty. The blade, what she could see, was sterling silver, and it contrasted sharply the blood that oozed around the entry wound and coagulated in her nightshirt.

The blood oozed slowly. Even though the blade was thick and long (she could feel it entirely within her, and she sensed it might pop out her back if she bent over), the wound did not gush. Rather, it leaked in the same way a neglected faucet bleeds water – one slow drop at a time.

Perhaps due to the slow rate of blood loss, she did not feel too weak to rise. She lifted herself out of bed and cried at the sight of herself in the mirror. She lamented the ache within her, but given her situation, she steeled herself toward her lot.

Outside of her room, her loving and supportive family awaited her. They were faithful, dedicated, and honorable people. They provided everything she needed to survive and succeed in the world, and they were there every day.

Her parents, both mother and father, were strapped to chairs and completely bound so that movement was impossible. She did not know how they sustained themselves, but they sat facing each other, and they suffered a condition in which their eyes were only capable of seeing each other. Their hearing was fine (they heard everything), and they spoke with eloquent, warm, and knowledgeable voices. But they reported that while they saw each other clearly, in beautiful vivid detail, in fact, everything else was merely a shade from which they could not distinguish one object from another.

Her other family – grandparents, aunts, uncles, cousins, nieces, nephews, in-laws, and siblings`– suffered the same ailments. They were similarly bound, and if married, had beautiful vision for their spouses, but were blind otherwise. All were aurally perceptive and profoundly articulate.

While all her family knew, talked with, and listened to her – indeed loved her without hesitation or condition – they were primarily occupied with existing. That is, she understood that the food she ate, the bed she slept in, the clothes she wore, were the product of their constant, sustained diligence. It was not selfish occupation. She understood that this was their love for her.

They engaged in their occupations mentally by methods that she could neither see nor understand. She knew they were hard at work by some of their utterances and overheard conversations, but how they contacted their employers or anyone outside of the house without leaving their chairs, and how this contact transformed to food, home, and garment, she never fathomed. She accepted them, their ways, and their love as it was given.

Incidentally, and inexplicably, perhaps due to her great admiration, love, and respect for her familiars, she kept her thoughts and feelings to herself. They toiled and provided, she lived relatively healthily and happily, and this was natural as she saw it. Her family accepted her this way, assuming all was well, and the system functioned.

She did not mention the dagger. She cleaned herself up and prepared for work as usual. These usual procedures were arduous, unclean, and difficult – she dared not remove the dagger for fear of her life – and work remained. Since she could not explain the appearance of the dagger, upon entering the room and hearing "hellos" from her family, and seeing them engaged and hard at work, she ate and left as normal.

Outside the world was as ever. People of all conditions populated her vision, and the city's structure was fixed. Even with a piece of off-white bone protruding from her mid-section, no one said a word.

Blood oozed as slowly as possible leaving great blotches of color upon her beautiful clothes, and puss and scabs and detritus of unknown sorts collected near the obvious. Proudflesh.

No one said a word.

On a street corner where she stood, she beheld a beauty and a bum not five feet apart. The bum lay supine in the gutter, feet swollen like hot sausages. The beauty swiveled and lifted her arms to brush aside her set, styled, blonde hair, and a man in a suit stopped to marvel. A driver skidded and lay on his horn at the man. The bum stirred and Maria noticed that he lived. The man in the suit yelled at the driver who gave him the finger and sped off. The man cursed him away and went over to the blonde and asked her name. She replied, "Miriam," and they began talking. Maria noticed that he was completely animated and making grand gestures with his arms and hands until he accidentally flailed his arms a bit too far and smacked the bone which protruded from Maria and sent a shrill of pain into her core. The bum groaned and labored to roll over and go to sleep or pass out or find some ounce of comfort that can be gotten at such a level. The man who had struck Maria snarled and said, "Excuse me," in an exaggerated way as if saying the words sent a pain into *his* core and the words could not be gotten rid of quickly enough – all while seeing the bone and the Maria's wince of pain. Maria stepped back.

No one said a word.

Co-workers at Maria's office looked and said nothing in particular and laughed amongst each other and ate and smiled and talked about their loved ones and always with opinions, never allowing the remote possibility of a hint or suggestion of self-doubt or humility or simple tolerance, as if the phrase "if you don't have anything nice to say don't say anything at all" was an offense punishable by murder.

No one said a word.

Blood oozed, and late in the day, she would stumble and fall, perhaps at the blood loss.

Still, no one said a word.

By four o'clock, when the most blood had been lost, and the dress was soaked, and her legs were tired, and she prayed for home, family, and bed, and everyone whom she met would avoid looking directly at the bone protruding from her body, would say nothing at all and with their cold blooded eyes and bitter smirks communicate, "Maria, there is nothing that you can show me that will make me feel sorry for you. We will not talk about it."

Maria went home. She cried. She suffered. Woe beset Maria from all directions in all shapes and sizes to the tune of black somber dirges with the look of funeral dark clothing and frowns for smiles and thoughts which cannot be mentioned as clear as crimson blood on a window pane with glazed rain on a cloudy, foggy, misty, cold, sunless, but watery day.

Poor Maria.

And the off-white bone handle of the exquisite and ornate dagger remained, plain enough for anyone to mention. It stayed and ached dully, persistently, and consistently until she accepted herself, dagger or not, despite what people would or would not say to her within or without her presence, but her family always loved and supported her and the flesh of her wound finally outgrew the handle and covered it and enclosed it and her belly swelled and people slowly began to look (but still not say) – "An unwedded pregnant girl?" – until she, after many years and many labors bore a beautiful daughter of her own and strangers and co-workers and bosses and friends and neighbors and all people said, "Maria, it is not fair that you are so fortunate and have such a beautiful baby. Talk to us about it."

Maria heard.

And considered.

But before any thought took hold, she heard within her mind the sound of her daughter crying and she knew that she had acquired the gift of her family, the thing that allowed them to touch the world without moving. And suddenly her vision transformed so that she could not see the strangers and co-workers and bosses and friends and neighbors, but only shades instead. And always, above their ceaseless din which was now inescapable, she heard her baby and knew that she was a mother and her work was cut out for her, so that she looked forward to returning home, the place of love, where she would only have eyes for the True.

Jack

Jack is 10 years older than I. I am no better than he. I didn't always think this way. When I met Jack, he was the leader of a group of guys that I carried water for. He laughed and joked and bragged and cut up and walked around with his belly hanging over his belt and his hair slicked back-like and a clean shave and sometimes a three piece suit or jeans and cross-trainer shoes; the guys all liked Jack and when he talked, they listened. I wasn't usually part of the huddle, but within earshot nonetheless, I heard him.

"Can I sit in the closet and watch?" That was one of his favorite sayings. All the guys laughed. Even after he said it 100 times, someone laughed. I wasn't sure what it meant, but I imagined.

I was a serious boy. I carried water. Being slightly built, it wasn't an easy job, but my arms learned how to do it. Five gallon buckets full of water are heavy, but I learned to move. From the source to the guys and back to the source again, all day long, I served. They drank and laughed. Always, "Can I sit in the closet and watch?", and the men laughed.

Of course there were moments of respite. In those times, I would mind my own business. It didn't matter if I was near the guys or not, I would keep my nose down, and steel myself for the next round of to and from. And always, Jack talked. And the men replied. I listened.

Occasionally, Jack would turn his eye toward me. "Hey Farmer, how's it going?" I would nod recognition, sometimes make brief eye contact, but in those days I found it easier to stare downwards. Jack made jokes to me, but I only knew they were jokes because he didn't raise his voice or demand I do something. I can't repeat any single one because I simply don't remember. And seeing me sit there, locked down, Jack would finally say, "Hey, Farmer." And I would look because I had to. Dig? And he would say, "Farmer, you are not the only one."

I didn't know what to make of that. I didn't know what he meant or what I should say. All I knew was that Jack was tough and I was not and he could say things to me that I didn't understand and to which I did not know how to reply. It was weird.

In truth, I hated Jack. He was a bastard. He was the son of a bastard. Jack ran the show, I carried water, and everybody loved Jack. I hated the fucker. His stupid fucking jokes: "Can I sit in the closet and watch?"

I eventually put in enough time and left. I stopped carrying water and moved on to something else. It was better, but I always remembered Jack. Jack fucked who he wanted, when he wanted. "Can I sit in the closet and watch?"

I hated the fucker. Hated, hated, hated. Fucker, fuck, fuck. But as time passed and I grew older, I began dreaming of the things that I had heard him talking about.

In my sleeping hours, I watched all types of blue movies in which Jack was the star and I was…sitting in the closet and watching. And I woke from the dreams screaming. It hit me. I understood what he had been saying.

"Can I sit in the closet and watch?"

And I realized that Jack had done the things that I had only thought about. I wanted to be Jack.

But Jack was long gone – off to Timbuktu or God only knows where, slugging it out, livin' the best he knew how.

And so am I.

I am a hypocrite. Come to realize that I am the worst kind – the kind who insists that he is not even when 99 people say he is.

So maybe there is still time. Jack is long gone, but Greg is the boss now. Greg is 10 years older than I am, too. Greg is tough and mean and dirty and makes the men laugh and is the center of attention. And when he talks, I listen. But now I have compassion for the Greg and Jacks of the world because I understand it is not easy maintaining his position. Greg's words are music to my ears even when I do not understand or agree with what he is saying. I do not judge him.

I'm OK with Greg and Jack. We are three of a kind.

Fathers and Sons

It is a cold day in Minneapolis and my father and I have met for a beer.

"Cold day," I say.

"Sure is," he replies.

I've been in Minneapolis for five years. I moved here to take a corporate job in finance. It wasn't my first choice, but it was an opportunity and I took it.

My dad lives in Maryland and does government work. He and my mom separated a long time ago and he hasn't remarried. He has dated a string of women – young women, women his age, rich women, poor women, career women, single mothers, married women – the works. I guess after being with mom so long, he needs to sow his wild oats. I don't hold it against him. I am not married, and I don't much care to be, either. I can understand why a man doesn't want to be married.

"Who's playing?" he asks.

"Notre Dame versus Nebraska."

"Who you putting your money on?"

"I'm for the fighting Irish," I say. "They're closer."

"Closer?" he asks.

"Closer to where I live," I reply.

"Well, I guess I'm for Nebraska then," he grins.

We talk awhile. He tells me what he's up to in Maryland. He asks me how often I talk to mom and whether or not I'm close with my sister. He says he's proud of her, hopes things work out for her and her husband in Florida. Says he never was sure about that guy, but that if she loves him, then he's behind her 100%.

I mention that mom's well and she's really happy with the remodeling job they did on the house. He smiles without looking at me, says "good," and lifts his beer.

We sit in silence for a bit and watch Notre Dame and Nebraska tangle. It's a deadlock. All defense – nobody moves the ball.

A couple of nice college-age women walk in and take a seat at the end of the bar. They are rapt in conversation and take no notice of their surroundings other than to order two cosmopolitans from the bartender.

Dad turns to me and asks, "Which one you like?"

"I like the dark-haired one with glasses and ivory skin," I say in a low voice.

"Really?" he asks. "I always figured you for a blonde kind of guy."

"Why's that?"

"Well, see, I'd take the blonde one. Plump ample breasts and backside, long blonde hair, and olive skin, even on a cloudy day in Minneapolis." He looks at me and grins. "She's just my type."

I look him right back, and it is right then I realize that we are not interested in the same woman.

Minority Schizophrenic

Now.

There are no more than 1% of me.

I am nobody. I am everybody. I am anybody. It doesn't matter. Call me whatever whoever you want. I don't care. If anger is before or here or after anywhere ever inspired, I am not your problem. I don't matter.

<u>I am better than you are.</u>

<u>I am better than you are better.</u>

There are 99% of you.

You are not a minority to me.

Your troubles, no matter how loudly you shout, are meaningless. Compared to me, it is not worth it that you try.

There are so many of you that you make a simple majority seem like a single black sheep in a 1000 sheep herd. I will not bother to explain majorities. The question insults me. Look it up book Internet anyway your imagination points when forced – ask someone – Figure it out.

      You are a whiner. Your protestations, lamentations; your troubles bring shame upon you and yours simply because there are more of you than there are of me and your failure to realize this makes you a stooge and anybody not you sees this. The louder you cry the clearer it becomes. Your stubborn insistence makes the audience laugh louder, and *are you waiting* until you are the last one and absolutely everyone knows so that even the Devil's bitch is smiling and there is simply no way you cannot see yourself that you are the Dunce? For visualization's sake, it is like complaining that your food is not warm when everyone in the room is serving you. "Oh, the humanity!" i.e., grossticity.

Your problems mean nothing.
      You are not a minority.
      I am no more than 1% and you are more and you lose.
      Always.
      I beat you.
      You cannot win.
      I have already won.
      I am on the verge of laughing at your position…

This is real time.

———————————

Postscript: Did you think this was the end?

Of course there are others who are no more than 1%.

I am not the only one. ("Hey, Farmer.")

What about other minority groups?

Generally those of us at or under 1% are more concerned with obtaining the right for simple acceptance and the right to love openly and stand side by side in public without taking a 2 x 4 to the head or getting murdered point blank. Our struggle is worthy of everyone's respect including mine and especially yours because that situation is something to behold and learn from.

The farther down the scale below 1% you go the more awesome the spectacle. 0.75%, 0.67% 0.5%, 0.35%, 0.25% to fractions of a percent of a percent, the struggle is not even for acceptance – that is a spectacular dream for the Life Beyond – the struggle is for mere *recognition* – dig? – the acknowledgement that I exist, that I am here, regardless of how I am so openly ignored with prejudice and lied to by good, plain, and decent folks who insist that I am not what I so clearly am and appear to be, right on down the line to 1 person against everyone else, which percentage equals 1 divided by the total population of the world – ONE, in any language or symbol, against all the others – how's that for minority? – 1 against all – everyone's voice is a disgrace against themselves for the insistence that they are somehow more important than ONE, that they are entitled, that entitlement is a right, because someone wrote that – *Are you fucking kidding me?* – every day one is born who never tastes a morsel of food because they are entitled to what? and they die because their entitlement went down someone else's pipe and came out their luxury item – won't bother explaining – look it up book Internet – go ask someone – Figure it out.

Post Postscript: Numbers, or did you <u>still</u> think this was the end?

Any jackass half-awake or stoned during math class; indeed, any Joe or Joe-mama half-awake or stoned during United States knows that statistics are all about the characteristics used to create the statistics so that The Ultimate Evil One can be made to be the minority and therefore manipulated into being felt sorry for by everyone else in the majority. If someone lumps you in a majority and you figure out that majorities are for simple-minded fucks and command no sympathy from others and you want to find a minority to ally with so that you too can be sympathetic to others – the position of sympathy is powerful when the majority can no longer bear the guilt of their stubborn domination – just add more characteristics to your definition and watch your percentage plummet – you can travel from 75% to 5% in seconds – you can create new boxes and check all of them and you will be entitled right along with everyone else – for ultimate sympathy, insist on DNA testing which will scientifically show that you are one, an Army of One if you will, and then the entitlement clause will lift you to the top – and then you will have won, you will have succeeded, your dream will have come true – because you know that everyone is a unique individual and there is no one on planet Earth quite like you– "The Philosophy of United States," i.e., "Self-Reliance," R.W. Emerson, circa 1850 C.E.

And consider it a moment – take up the flag of faith or reason and you will arrive at the same conclusion because either way you go, either everyone everything came from God in any religion or any language or the universe started in one Big Bang from a singularity and furthering this concept according to some scientists either continues infinitely forever in this universe or contracts back to a singularity and repeats infinitely forever – the point is infinity anyway you go – it all comes from 1 ONE in any language or symbol – The Grand Ultimate Minority.

But wait – whoever said that minority = sympathy anyway? I'll bet The World Billionaires Club constitutes less than 1% of the total population. "Sympathy for the minority" logic dictates that they command sympathy, no?; for minorities should always be felt sorry for, right? But don't mistake my irony, for these Jacks are hot targets for members of the majority who wish they could be in their place– it's alotta pressure up top – Feel sorry for that, for their exposure allows the rest of us to slip through relatively easily – and question eagerness to be on top, for, *you want the gun pointed at you?* – But I'm not sayin' sympathy 'em, I'm sayin' "why you fussin'?"

Under the rules of duality, you can either hoist a gun or not. Get mad; but what are you going to do? What is your choice?

There you have it. The conductor of this train has done his job. He drives the train. You are all passengers and while you are making merry or having gastrointestinal problems in the loo, he is looking ahead to see if objects are on the track so that the train doesn't derail. He knows what he is for. There is nothing left to _____.

Minority Rising

There is a change in the air. A sea change. It is in the wind. If you listen, you can hear it. It is something like, "…the first one now, will later be last." Minority rising.

They are saying: "Hey look at me." "Don't shit on me." They are tired of the same old crap. "Why shouldn't we be on top? Why should we accept things the way they are?" I can't think of an argument which puts anyone inherently on top of another.

The tide is rising.

You can hear this all around you. It's not hard. You just have to listen.

"Drums. Drums in the deep."

"Get the hell out of here!"

If you hear them coming, you wanna stick around to see what they're packing?

Hell, I'll grant you, you *can* stick around to look if that floats your boat.

But ask yourself, what do I really know about someone by looking? You can never be sure what someone is really thinking until you ask him. Eyes lie. Both ways. Coming and going. That is, you don't know by looking into their eyes whether or not they are lying to you unless you have listened to them for awhile, and your own eyes can deceive you besides.

Dig?

Gentle Reader, you must understand that vision is not my forte. I have beautiful blue eyes but I am the walking blind. I hear voices. I remember voices. I cannot paint you a picture with the full color palette – blue, green, orange, magenta, red, purple, chartreuse, goldenrod, olive, candy-apple red, etc.

I am schizophrenic. I hear fucking people talking in my head.

I am having difficulty just show don't telling you a story in which a named character fully bloomed travels from point A to destination B having adventures in sequence along the way, meeting and having relationships with a host of other important and unimportant characters, illustrating all the time in full Technicolor the various elements of drama which could be setting, mood, attitude, time, conflict, while using metaphor, allusion, imagery, and every other bell and whistle for putting the picture in your head.

I am here to tell you that if you await visual confirmation, it will be too late. Sound isn't even in the same league as light but it is much closer to what we are as humans. At ~796mph, it is much closer to terra firma than light will ever be.

If you love your vision so much, why don't you go become a theoretical physicist? Get off on images from the Hubble telescope.

By the time you have visual confirmation, whatever you have waited for will have you right where it wants you and there will be no escape. Light travels at ~186,000 mps (second). That is *many* times faster than sound. I am not a scientist nor a mathematician.

Don't you know that sound is light's bitch?

By the time the Speed of Light catches you, you will be SOL. The Speed of Sound is not even a blip on SOL's radar. If SOL catches you, it is too late to send an SOS.

Dig?

Most wild animals – bears, gorillas, wildcats, wolves, and others – rely on their sense of hearing to stay clear of predators. They learned a long time ago that it is much easier to avoid the fucker than to tangle with him in the first place. Most of the time, you never see them. They stay safe and out of sight so that they may live to see another day.

In Kodiak, Alaska, it behooves you to walk with bells on your backpack.

Did you ever have the experience where you were resisting, being stubborn as it were, and your enemy looked you in the eyes and said, "This is the way it is," and the awful truth of it all was so painful that you didn't want to believe it? You, in fact, refused to believe it. And did you dig years later that he or she was right and the visual confirmation burned in your brain of he or she towering over you, sitting on you, fucking you, straight dominating you bitch as it were because "This is the way it is" was your proof?

Why didn't you listen the first time?

Narcessus

In the bizarro world, he is Narcissus's evil twin. He is the boy who never looks at himself in the mirror. He avoids mirrors of all sorts. Narcessus never looks at himself period. His reflection repels him. He refuses to believe anyone around him.

"Why don't you ever believe me, Narcessus?"

"Have some self-awareness, for cryin' out loud."

Narcessus is a one way circuit. He's all output. Twenty years on the same road and he has no idea where he is.

Color Blind

Back in 1982 I tried to buy a dress for my wife. We were on the outs. Some fight or another. I don't remember exactly. You know how husbands and wives fight about nothing, but it's everything? Like that.

Anyway, we were having problems. It was near Valentine's Day and I thought I'd buy her a dress instead of the usual flowers to show her that I really loved her and was thinking about her even though we were fighting and I was just trying to smooth things over in general.

My wife is real big on details. And I'm a dumb shit on that kind of stuff. I mean, as long as I hit the ballpark, I'm cool. But for my wife, it you don't walk away remembering that the seats were green and not blue, or that it was sunny without a cloud in the sky, then you are big jerk. She says that paying attention to details is love and for some reason her details always involve color.

I dig it, man. We've been married a long time now and I understand how to choke the engine properly if I want to get it running, and in the end that's all I really care about, is making sure the engine is running. I don't care if the seats are green or blue.

So we were fighting near Valentine's Day in '82 and I thought a nice dress was a relationship bull's eye. So I went to the department store and started up with the salesman.

I found a dress that looked really nice, and it was finely spun cotton like she likes, and the skirt part of it wasn't too high or low like she likes, and it would be real cool for going out to dinner and a play or something. And it was blue which is her favorite color.

I'm talking with the salesman explaining my predicament and he laughs about the situation until I mention the color. He says no, that isn't blue. It's black. I say, you're joking, that's blue. He says, no I'm not. It's straight black. I say you're wrong, because I'm not blind, thank you very much. So he says OK.

He rings me up and I stare at the thing for awhile insisting that it's blue.

I tell him again and he just shakes his head.

I walk away feeling pretty good. It's for my wife, I know what color she likes – she told me – blue – and I bought this thing for her because we are in a fight and I'm going to make things right and I'll be damned if some salesman is telling me different. I know I'm right.

I take the dress home. I am all set to give it to her after dinner when we start fighting again. I lose my temper and I think I even call her a "bitch." Needless to say she walks out of the room and V-Day is ruined.

I take a drive to cool off and when I get home I find my wife watching TV. Her makeup is still running from her eyes and I feel very bad for what I have done. I run up to our bedroom and pull out the gift box with the dress in it.

I am absolutely positively sure that this will make up for things. I got her a nice dress that is her favorite color.

When I give it to my wife on Valentine's Day she is less than thrilled. She smiles and makes a sigh and says, "Oh Robert, that was a very nice thought of you. A black dress for Valentine's Day. How appropriate."

I get furious. I can't believe the sales jack-ass was right. I swore that it was blue, OK, maybe navy blue, but blue nonetheless. It was no use arguing with my wife that night. I had already screwed the pooch too much.

It began to dawn on me that my vision wasn't too good.

We divorced five years later due to irreconcilable differences. My biggest lesson from that relationship was that I can't tell my ass from a hole in the ground. Literally.

I do not believe what I see.

I hear. I do not see.

The Struggle for…Happiness?

Bring it on home. Minority rising. Welcome the change. "The first ones now will later be last…" There is not enough time nor is it even possible for this reporter to enumerate or give recognition to all the minorities of the world even if she would like to – all nations all colors religions creeds sexes sexualities disabilities abilities those who have been clearly wronged by others. But she vociferously advocates their struggle for however they would define it, for it is up to them to define it for themselves. That is a right in United States. She would like nothing more than for everyone to be happy. She is expecting. What the heck else do all mothers want? Happiness for her children.

It is not for her to take up the implement of aggression i.e. weapon and shed the blood. Used to be a day that the men protected the village camp whatever in any tongue and the women held the rest together. "Those were happier times." Simpler in general all the way around. But all those women knew that what the men did was necessary. They trusted.

Struggle.

Funny thing. Struggling for happiness is like killing for peace. How can one work for fun? That is backwards. True fun is what one doesn't have to work at.

Work is great. It is necessary, but it is *always* work. What makes one sweat might be enjoyable but it raises the heart rate and the heart does double-time and it eventually wears out like a solid block engine. Call it what you want; label it anyway as exercise or healthy lifestyle but if one were to operate on double-time 24/7, then one would reduce one's total lifespan for sure. Fun, rest, relaxation is admitting that there is a time to be slobby and to relax, and sure, death is coming, but one need not *run* all the time.

The struggle for happiness with which everyone seems so deadly serious when talked about in public is a contradiction in terms that ought to be analyzed. The best medicine that this mother/reporter knows of is called, "Open up a big can of 'lighten up.'" Life is not all work, blood, warfare, and torture. Together, black and white can make beautiful music to which anyone can dance.

So, children. Mom knows that you all fight for what you think is right, and she blesses and prays for you because you are her children no matter what mischief you commit. And always, she is at home, wishing that you remember her.

Astro Boy

"Astro 1. This is operator 82 of GAIA Mission Control. How are you this fine day? Coordinates?"

It is the operator. I never know who it is, who it was, or who it will be. Sometimes it is a man. Sometimes it is a woman. They tell me they work in shifts. It is the same conversation each time.

"Alright," I say.

"Coordinates and velocity?"

I am a pilot for the Good Adventures for Inquisitive Astronauts program – GAIA. It is the space research arm of a coalition of the Great Governments Space Colonization Effort (GGSCE). The governments of GGSCE decided to look for other habitable systems, or failing that, life in outer space, at least. They put together the technology and assembled a space craft capable of quick travel. They held tryouts among the top educated military pilots worldwide for the pilot most qualified to operate the craft and carry out the mission.

The idea is that if we find other life in space, perhaps they will help us further propagate our own species. If we find other habitable systems, then humans can begin moving, en masse, into outer space.

The tryouts came down to a shootout between me and my counterpart, and we were equally matched in all ways except that my vision was slightly better than 20/20 and hers was not. They let her break the bottle on the bow of my ship and promised to let her take the next one.

"2 parsecs from Betelgeuse system. 43,000 mps," I say.

On the day of my departure, the President charged me with my mission in front of the all the world's press. He said something like, "Young man, you are mankind's hope for the future. Your efforts will lead us into an age of new light, and you will stand among such greats as Neil Armstrong. We are all counting on you." I smiled and shook his hand, but I watched the cameras.

The situation on earth is intensifying like an autoclave without a pressure release. The GGSCE is earth's unified purpose for a future.

"Good work, Astro 1. This is operator 82 signing off. Another operator will be checking in presently. 'Go strongly into the future.'"

"Go strongly…" Ha. That was the President's new motto.

I am mankind's hope for the future. He told me so. But all I do is send reports. I am a tool.

But not anymore. Not today. I *always* send the reports. They have counted on me.

But this is the last one.

I'm tired of the operators. I'm tired of the mission. When they selected me, they said that my better than 20/20 vision was the sole reason for my appointment. They said that anyone with my qualifications plus a gift like that was specially made for this job. They said that I was a fine representative of the GGSCE.

They will soon know that this is my last transmission. I'm never answering the COM again. I'm not going back. I stole DNA and cloning technology – enough to start my own colony. I have enough literature and books, food…whatever. I don't need humanity, nor do I want it.

Boy, I would like to see the look on their faces. By that time, my counterpart ought to be have started her own mission. I will be a write-off.

I always had this in mind. I never wanted their stupid mission. As soon as I saw my way off that rock, I took it. Lucky for me I had enough covers to make it past the screens. Otherwise I would not have had the option. I was always dissatisfied with the conditions on Earth, and as soon as I realized that I had the ability to get off, I took it.

If I meet new life – cool. Something interesting. If habitable ground, then I will start my own world.

If I just fly around until the end, no problem. I had long made up my mind before revealing my plans. I am not worried about them and by the time they figure out what happened, it will be too late to reach me.

And as the bliss of my genius begins to spread from my brain to my limbs, and I start to ease the seat of the cockpit back and put my dogs up on the dash, I am suddenly jarred awake: "Wake up, Farmer!"

I nearly curse at my embarrassment.

"Sleeping on the job again?" Greg asks. He is the boss. He just shakes his head and walks away.

I shake my own head to clear the cloudiness. I stand up.

I was dreaming. I thought I was Astro Boy.

I am still the water boy.

I carry water.

MRS

"The next person to say that people who commit suicide are cowards or that suicide is the easy way out defaults his or her rights and automatically signs up for *My Reality Show*. *MRS* does not last for 30 days. You do not get to eat rare foods or perform acrobatics or feats of strength in controlled conditions where the risk of getting hurt is effectively nil. You do not get to live amongst friends or strangers in a major city. You do not get to compete with fellow contestants in any way using mind or matter. Joining *MRS* means saying goodbye to everything you know and love. This includes the spouse and significant other you cherish, the dependents you adore, the places that make you feel good, anything you enjoy such as reading or watching TV or swimming, anything you possess; in short, the experience of *MRS* will force you to live in discomfort 100% of the time.

"There are only two ways off the show and there are no short cuts because you can't cheat on *MRS*. I control *MRS* and you can't beat me. I know everything before you do.

"The point of *MRS*, and the main way off the show, is that you have to want to kill yourself. As I mentioned, there is absolutely no way to short-circuit this stipulation. Pretending only extends the length of your stay.

"On *MRS* you will willingly or unwillingly experience total ego breakdown until you are begging for death, and assistants will be standing by to offer gun, knife, rope, pills – whatever it takes to get the job done – for you to suicide yourself. And as you suck on the barrel of the gun, or grip the handle of the knife, or cinch the rope, or juggle the pills, you will begin to be asked, "Are you a coward for thinking of making your own way out?" by the assistants, and you will have to choose under this duress what is right for you.

"By our technological means, we will wipe this entire discussion from your head and you will not remember these parameters. As far as you will know, you will never see another thing or person you love again. You will want death or face the long long life of despair on *MRS*. That's the sum total of your choice.

"You will not remember that if you go through with it, the gun shoots blanks, the knife blade retracts, the 2lb. test rope breaks, and the pills are placebos. The assistants will parade you around while confetti and streamers fall from the ceiling. Lights, sirens, dwarves in mini cars, the whole bit. *MRS* ends and you return to everything you love.

"But you will not expect this. You will submit to your death because you really want to die and there is no other way.

"For those of you who are saying, 'Fuck you man! I'll fake you out. I don't have to listen to you, you faggot! At the very least I'll wait it out to the bitter end and prove you wrong,' I say, 'That's mighty tough of you.' But remember, you have already forfeited your rights and there is nothing you can do. If you do live your whole long life in despair on *MRS*, I'll shake your hand on your death bed and say I hope it was worth it when you could have just admitted that the cause of suicide is personal and relative to the person that feels it and no one else is fit to judge them because given the right set of unrelenting circumstances anyone is capable of the deed and no one is better than anyone else and you could have returned to all that you love, happy and compassionate and more sensitive to everything that's good on Earth. And I'll release your hand

and piss on you before you die because that's what tough cats do to each other.

"'Good job, Impervious!'"

> Note: *Some of those who kill*
> *themselves are less*
> *selfish than others,*
> *and it is their very*
> *inability to give*
> *themselves what*
> *others willingly take*
> *that causes them to*
> *leave in the first*
> *place.*

Dig?

R.I.P. KB, Feb 2007

O & E

Anybody knows that Orpheus was passionate. He was a lover and a musician. Not a general, not a merchant, not an attorney, not a judge, not a counselor, not a teacher. He was a man who wore his heart on his sleeve, collar, and cap and a lyre on his back.

He traveled Hades to reclaim his beloved Eurydice. Dig? He went *underground* for her. He went to Hell for her. He went downtown to the Land of Darkness for her.

Now, I'm no expert, but I'm pretty sure that the Land of the Dead is not a fun place to be, but Orpheus was the type of guy willing to go. For her.

He ran down with his heart on his sleeve, collar, and cap and his lyre on his back, fearless with the single purpose of Eurydice on his mind. Any beloved should be so lucky.

And when he got her, he led them both back to Earth and made the deal not to look at her as he until she had cleared the underworld.

Fearlessly and enthusiastically, Orpheus led her on, with his heart on his sleeve, collar, and cap and his lyre on his back and a smile on his face. Wouldn't you with all that requited love and your beautiful princess at your heels?

When he cleared the Gates of Hell, he emerged in the bright sunlight and he knew he was home. The dead were gone and he recognized the trees and mountains and grass and animals that he had temporarily left behind. He smelled the cool, crisp air and tasted it on his lips. He felt the exuberance of life.

He turned to welcome his beloved Eurydice in his arms. *My love*, he would say, *we are finally safe*.

Eurydice had not cleared the Gates. Being slightly slower and having fallen just a bit behind, she lingered at the entrance. When Orpheus turned, she vanished and said, "Farewell." It echoed in the valley.

He fell to his knees and looked without speaking. His eyes watered up and he just stared. The echo stayed in his brain. And as he fathomed what had happened, the blood rushed to his face making him appear cranberry red, and the tears steamed away, and he beat the grass with his fists: "Why why why?" he screamed and when his fists were bruised purple he ripped the lyre from his back and smashed it to pieces. The heart on his sleeve, collar, and cap and the lyre on his back oozed crimson blood.

It was rumored that after he recovered, he pickled himself in bitterness and used his musical talents to seduce unwary females for whom he felt nothing as he had for his beloved Eurydice. "Farewell."

Poor Orpheus. Lover and singer. He had the fruit only to discover that by the time he ate it, it was bitter.

It occurs to this researcher that this incident could have been avoided, yet the myth makes no mention of an alternative. Wouldn't it have seemed logical for Orpheus to have allowed Eurydice to give him some signal before he looked back for her? Something like, "Hey Orpheus, lookamee." Or, "Hey Phee, come n' get it." Or, simply, "Orpheus, I am clear of the underworld and it is safe for you to look now," at which point Orpheus would've turned and seen his beloved Eurydice and they would've embraced and kissed and caressed and felt relieved and the fruit he had obtained would've remained sweet and not turned bitter after all.

Poor Orpheus.

Reckoning Day

…Farmer wakes up from his Astro Boy dream.

So it is my turn at the podium. Recollect an elder once saying, "What would you say to everyone if you had your 15 minutes?" Well, this is it.

My fluffer straightens my lapel, pats my shoulders, and says, "Go gettum, Adrian. Smile big."

And then it is the MC: "Next up is a young man all the way from Seattle, Washington, Adrian Francis Farmer."

The fluffer kicks my ass stagewards.

I enter the auditorium to a standing ovation. 10,000 fans, friends, participants – the audience, I mean – laud me. And then they take their seats in silence.

I begin: "Rise sound junkies, rise. Show those vision addicts who's boss. While they are awaiting visual confirmation at 186,000 mps, tell them, "Hello, I love you. I am your friend; I've been here all along," and when they pretend they don't hear, those stupid fucks, zooming around at nearly the speed of light, smash your microphones over their heads; hurl the amplifiers over your head like Hercules – "Do you see that motherfucker?" – and have a friend film it and after they are hospitalized with concussions – the Kinesthetic Fix – send them the video across the wire at the speed of light with an audio recording attached – Do you see that motherfucker? – that says, "Goodbye", the opposite of hello – let them try to figure that one out; and start your reprise sound junkies; a soft ballad with a simple voice over a stringed instrument that says everything you ever wanted to say but that they were too deaf to listen to; it is heard; it is accomplished."

And when I finish my final sentence, my final glorious ending for which I have been waiting my whole life, I miss the glorious flourish and fanfare. No applause. Nothing. Not even a smile. In fact, it is now that I recognize General Biggamee in my peripheral vision. He is standing at attention and blowing a whistle.

The 10,000 are standing up in formation. Men, women, and children first are hoisting firearms. It appears the children have handguns, the ladies shotguns, and the men high-powered rifles with enormous scopes. I look toward my shoes and see my body lit brightly in laser red.

So it is a double-cross. It is a shit sandwich the likes I have never tasted. They don't call it Sloppy Joe for nothing. It can barely maintain its shape at this viscosity. But a shit sandwich all the same. No need to elaborate here. Dig? I am screwed. I get it.

[pause]

I turn back to my fluffer to ask, "Why? Why didn't you tell me?" but I see that he's already busy with the next contestant, guest, challenger…human being, I mean. I am on my own.

And I hear General Biggamee ask, "Why so surprised? Don't you know where you are? Who did you think you were?" And he smiles baring his teeth which are strangely sharp and glistening as if moist. "Don't you know that this is The Society of Perpetually Starving Cannibals? We've been expecting you."

I am fucked. I am out of moves and time. I am guilty of ignorance in the wrong part of town. There is nothing left to _____.

How did General Biggamee know when to speak when he did? Could he read my thoughts? Could he hear my mind? Could he feel my inner voice? Regardless.

He is raising the whistle to his mouth again.

The last thing I remember is my training. Someone once said, "Always have a fail safe plan," or was it, "Don't get caught with your pants down." There is so little time; I can't figure it out. Regardless.

Like a spy who reaches for his cyanide capsule after he is caught by the enemy, I reach around my waist to the small of my back right between and just above my glutes and draw my pistol. As General Biggamee puts the whistle in his mouth, puffs his cheeks, and raises his eyelids and brows, I put the gun in my mouth and pull the trigger. It is over.

--Last words of Adrian Francis Farmer 6 April 2007

Hello Mama

After becoming lonely, tired, and depressed, although not in that order, I kicked back my recliner and took a nap only to be awoken 1000 years later by the woman of my dreams. She had long dark hair, deep brown eyes, smooth white skin over a soft, kind face, and an expression of joy which made me want to cry. And when she saw my eyes fill with water, she brushed her open hand against my cheek, smiled, and asked, "What's wrong?" I said, "I was lonely, tired, and depressed, and I lay down to rest, and while I slept, I dreamed. I dreamed that I was not lonely, not tired, not depressed. I dreamed of you, the beautiful woman of my dreams, and you became my friend. You said, 'Adrian, I am your friend. I will stay with you. I will listen to you and follow you. I will sit with you if you don't want to go anywhere.' Your words soothed me and I relaxed. I felt satisfied that my days of being alone were over. And the dream continued and we lived together for our entire lifetimes until we were both old. One night, as we both sat around a fire, you looked at me and said, 'Adrian, am I not your friend?' 'Yes,' I said. 'And do you believe that I will stay with you and listen to you and follow you and sit with you if you desire?' 'Yes,' I said again. 'Good,' you said. 'But Adrian, you must wake up now, for you have been dreaming.' And I stared, not wanting to believe you, but you got up and walked away. You left the room. I followed you but could not find you. I thought you deserted me. And before long I grew lonely, tired, and depressed until I sat down in my recliner and took a nap. The next thing I knew you were waking me up."

"Adrian, you silly boy. I have been here all along. You weren't sleeping. You weren't even lonely, tired, or depressed. You were dreaming with your eyes open."

And she was right.

Let Go My Ego

"Move along. Move along."
   Go to mall.
   Sit down.
   (Who is talking? To whom?)
   No subject. Can write a whole lot and say much
and show even more but how do you know who is doing it?
How do you know who you are talking to is really who he
or she says she is? How do you really know who you are?
How do you know anything?
   You or I or he or she or it or they or we could be the
subject. Subject is relative.
   You or me or him or her or it or them or us could be
the object. Object is relative. [analysis of preceding
sentence will indicate improper use of nouns *me, him, her,*
etc. in subject position]
   Subject and object are unimportant unless you insist
on absolute control. An unimportant subject does not
object to his or her removal, only his or her subjugation.
   "Nothing matters."
   Who is talking?

Last Words of Adrian Francis Farmer

(   ) know that English is symbol system only
can be turned around (it)
(k)no(w) meaning
now you see I now you don't
___ am or is fucking with you ☺
k(no)w self?

Epilogue, epilogue

"Depression and gratitude cannot co-exist."
        Thank you very much.
        "Can't complain."